COLIN
the Cart Horse

For Nia & Rhys – GP

First published in 2016
by Faber and Faber Limited
Bloomsbury House
74–77 Great Russell Street
London WC1B 3DA

Designed by Faber and Faber
Printed in Malta

Text © Gavin Puckett, 2016
Illustrations © Tor Freeman, 2016

The right of Gavin Puckett and Tor Freeman to be identified as author
and illustrator of this work respectively has been asserted in
accordance with Section 77 of the
Copyright, Designs and Patents Act 1988

978–0571–31543–7

2 4 6 8 10 9 7 5 3 1

COLIN
the Cart Horse

Gavin Puckett

Illustrated by Tor Freeman

ff

FABER & FABER

Hello young reader . . . !

Thanks for taking the time,
In selecting my book of ridiculous rhyme.
I'm Gavin, (you'll find my full name on
      the cover)
The teller of tales, which you're soon to
      discover.
It's taken me years to unearth these
      strange fables,
By visiting farmyards and hanging round
      stables
– And this is a series with just a selection,
      of some of the weirdest in my
      collection.

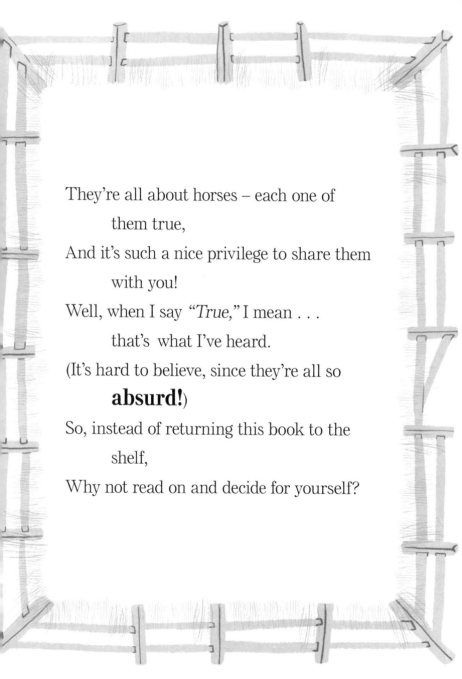

They're all about horses – each one of
  them true,
And it's such a nice privilege to share them
  with you!
Well, when I say *"True,"* I mean . . .
  that's what I've heard.
(It's hard to believe, since they're all so
  absurd!)
So, instead of returning this book to the
  shelf,
Why not read on and decide for yourself?

Colin had worked for most of his life

And had been a good servant to Will

  and his wife.

He ploughed through the meadows, pulled

  carts through the field

And helped every summer to harvest

  the yield.

Will's kids ADORED him and so did their

dad –

He was simply the best horse this farm

EVER had!

They rode on his cart through the wind,

snow and rain,

And they helped clean his stable and

groomed Colin's mane.

Colin loved work, it was clear to see,

And he grafted each weekday from seven

'til three.

The farmer was grateful and paid him

each day

With stack-upon-stack of DELICIOUS

fresh hay.

Hay was his favourite, he found it

a treat.

It was ever so soft and remarkably sweet.

At breakfast time,
Colin would
have a quick
MUNCH,

Then pause
around twelve
and have hay
for his lunch.

6

Then when work had
    finished (just
        after three),
Colin walked to his
    stable and ate
        some for tea.

Even for supper, he **LONGED** for a snack,
And grazed on a bale as he lay on his back.

Colin was thankful for all that he had,

He was awfully happy and ever so glad.

But Colin didn't realise that Will had a need,

For giving his horse this particular feed.

The farmer used hay and his horse in

conjunction,

To naturally trigger a bodily function.

This process occurred deep inside

Colin's belly –

Creating a substance quite **squidgy** and

SMELLY.

It was gooey and pooey, but wholesome

and pure.

The name of this stuff . . . ? Why, of course

- it's MANURE!

Horse dung is fruitful, fertile and clean,

And Colin's manure was the best Will

had seen!

It fertilized, it fed, it nurtured and

nourished,

And any plant touched by it flowered and

flourished.

The farmer grew vegetables, all shapes

and sizes.

He took part in contests and often won

prizes.

So when Will '*MUCKED OUT*,' he'd

always ensure

That he kept every ounce of this

precious manure.

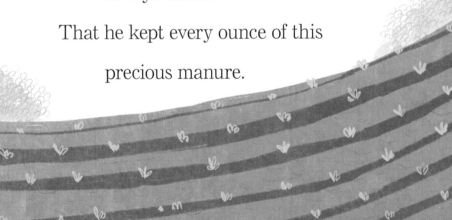

He spread it each day, all over his crops,

It was better than any stuff bought from

the shops!

But even though Colin admired his hay,

Quite often his daydreams and thoughts

    went *ASTRAY.*

The horse felt a curious question repeating,

Concerning the livestock and what

    they were eating.

He pondered at work; he mused in his bed.

Curiosity plagued him and badgered

    his head.

He questioned and quizzed 'til it made his

brain rattle . . .

What did Will feed to the rest of the

cattle?

16

One day at the farm, on Colin's day off.

The horse saw some pigs with their heads in

a trough.

He ambled on over, quite eager to see,

Just what these piggies were eating for tea.

Colin delivered his usual greeting;

Then asked the pigs, "What are you eating?"

One of the animals lifted its head,

It chomped and it slobbered . . .

   "Pellets!" it said.

The little brown pellets looked ever

   so **scrummy**,

And set off a rumble inside Colin's tummy.

"Can I try some?" asked Colin, with a
mischievous grin.

"Of course!" said the pig, "Come on over –
tuck in!"

The horse **bolted over** with vigour and
haste;

Then gave a sniff before having a taste.

The pellets were crunchy and
tasted delicious.

"Eat up . . ." said the pig, "They're
very nutritious!"

Colin obliged as the piggy looked on,

And in no time at all, the pellets

were gone.

"OUTSTANDING!" said Colin,

"Have a nice day."

He waved to the pigs and then went on

his way.

Colin strolled on feeling rather content,

Then passing the henhouse, he picked

up a scent.

He noticed the chickens all gathered around,

A mountain of corn that they pecked from
the ground.

He stopped for a moment to speak with

the fowl,

But the sweet-smelling corn caused his

tummy to **GROWL**.

"Can I try some?" asked Colin as he entered

the pen.

His chicken friend clucked. "Of course!" said

the hen.

Colin knelt down and he had a quick taste,

Then GOBBLED THE LOT, leaving no

corn to waste.

"Delightful!" scoffed Colin,

 "That was **sublime**!"

His chicken friend winked,

 "That's OK, anytime."

Colin set off, ready for bed;

Then he noticed the cows standing next to

 their shed.

He trotted on over and saw right away,

A large pile of vegetables placed in

 their tray.

"Good evening!" said Colin, "Those veggies
look great!"
As he ***licked*** both his lips at the thought of
a plate.

"Can I try some?" asked Colin, (for the

THIRD time that night).

He stood there in silence, 'til a bull

said . . . "Alright."

"Fab!" said the horse (then goodness knows

how)

He managed to **squeeze** himself

next to the cow.

Once in the line, he knelt on a ledge,

Where he chewed and he chomped on the

cows' tasty veg.

"That was lovely!" said Colin, his tummy
now full,
"Thank you!" he neighed. "Goodbye,"
moo'd the bull.

The horse trundled home, back to

his place,

With a look of **ACHIEVEMENT** all over

his face.

It had been a remarkable end to the

day . . .

Having realised . . . there **IS** more to

life than just hay!

The following morning, the horse rose

from bed

And cantered to work, leaving Will

at the shed.

The farmer began his familiar routine

And mucked out the stable until it

was clean.

But as the man shovelled, emptied and

cleared,

He sensed something **strange**. The

manure seemed **weird**!

The dung appeared heavy, quite bulky
and full.

Like something he'd normally get from
a bull.

Nevertheless, Will finished his chore,

And spread the muck over his veggies

once more.

Then, a little while later, (whilst his cattle

were grazing)

The farmer experienced something

AMAZING.

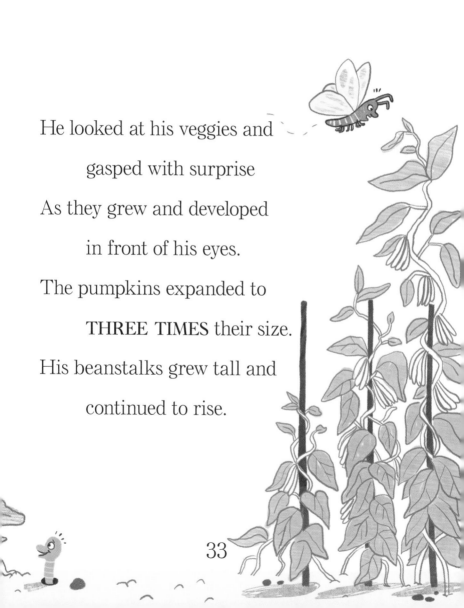

He looked at his veggies and
gasped with surprise
As they grew and developed
in front of his eyes.
The pumpkins expanded to
THREE TIMES their size.
His beanstalks grew tall and
continued to rise.

The carrot-tops stood, half a foot from

the ground,

And the onions – like **beach balls** –

were sizeably round.

This veg was enough to make ten

thousand dinners –

Or better still, entered as show-stopping

winners!

Farmer Will stood there rather

confused, then realised,

"IT MUST BE THE *MANURE*

I USED!"

But why is it different? Will asked in

his head.

What's so special about this muck that

I spread?

The farmer was **baffled** – and though it

was strange,

He was desperate to know what had

triggered this change.

To find out, he'd have to go straight

to the source –

To the creature who crafted it – Colin

the horse.

Will quickly found him, and asked right

away,

"Did you eat something, Colin – in addition

to hay?"

Colin felt nervous, but began to convey,

What he had eaten the previous day.

He felt quite **ASHAMED**, a little ungrateful,

And assured the farmer, "It was only a

plateful!"

Will was amazed. How could three simple

motions,

Result in such wonders of **EPIC**

proportions?

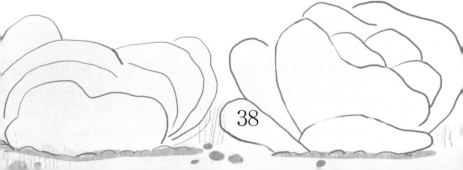

He thought of the wealth that this

substance could bring,

And how this could make him the

'GARDENING KING.'

But in order to get there, one thing was

for sure.

He'd need plenty more of this

SUPER-MANURE!

That's when he took the horse back to

the shed,

And stockpiled the foodstuffs that Colin

had said.

"Eat all you want." Will said full of smiles,

As he poured out the pellets and corn

into piles.

"I'll bring you some veggies, you can stay

here all day;

And make sure you mix them with plenty

of hay!"

Colin agreed, "Certainly Willie."

Then stayed in his stable – and

stuffed himself **silly**!

A few hours later (by quarter past four)

Colin was slumped in a heap on the floor.

He had gorged and devoured a

stupendous amount –

There were so many sacks that the

horse had LOST COUNT!

42

Too full to move, a muscle or sinew;

The happy horse smiled . . . Long may it

continue!

Just then, Colin's tummy started to

grumble,

It felt rather strange; not its usual rumble.

It whined and it curdled, it
bubbled and slurped.
Then Colin shot upright,
and suddenly burped.

BUUURP!

"Pardon me!" he exclaimed, in a

dignified way.

But another burp followed . . .

Only, this went ASTRAY!

Unlike most, this didn't come

from his mouth.

Oh no, it retracted, and

belched from down

south!

The noise was ferocious,

something of WONDER,

Which echoed so loud you could

swear it was *THUNDER*!

It silenced the place – the cows all stopped
mooing;
It distracted the others from what they
were doing.

There wasn't a sound, the farmyard

went flat –

And suddenly everyone asked . . .

"WHAT WAS THAT?"

Colin stood up full of shame and disgrace,

With a look of **EMBARRASSMENT** over

his face.

"How awful!" he cried, at his rather

strange turn.

Then he once again felt his insides start

to churn.

"Not again!" cried the horse with a

horrified fright,

And CLENCHED BOTH HIS BUTTOCKS with

all of his might.

But not even something as strong as

a horse,

Could do battle against this **MAGNIFICENT**

force!

This ripper roared louder, ferocious and fast;

Like ninety-nine motorbikes rocketing past!

The horse closed his eyes and felt

palpitations,

Whilst the noise **shook** the stable and

rocked its foundations.

Soon it was over, but could not

be forgotten;

It had left something ghastly,

disgusting and rotten.

Like an **odorous demon**

from the bowels of hell,

A tsunami of stench . . .

an UNSPEAKABLE smell!

The stink was **horrendous**, brutal
and hard.
It seeped through the window then
out to the yard.
It turned to a mist, impure and unclean –
That polluted the farmyard and made the
air GREEN.

The chickens all *fainted*,

as did the cows,

It was even too much for the

boars and the sows!

Then the vile, vicious vapour got

caught by the breeze,

Causing squirrels

and birds

to fall

out

from their trees!

The children both shouted, "Daddy . . .

let us in, quick!

Open the door . . . we're gonna be **sick**!"

Will told his wife, "Lock the windows and

doors!"

As he crawled to the stable and WHEEZED

on all fours.

"COLIN STOP EATING!" Will yelled with

a **SHRIEK**,

Holding his nose as he started to speak.

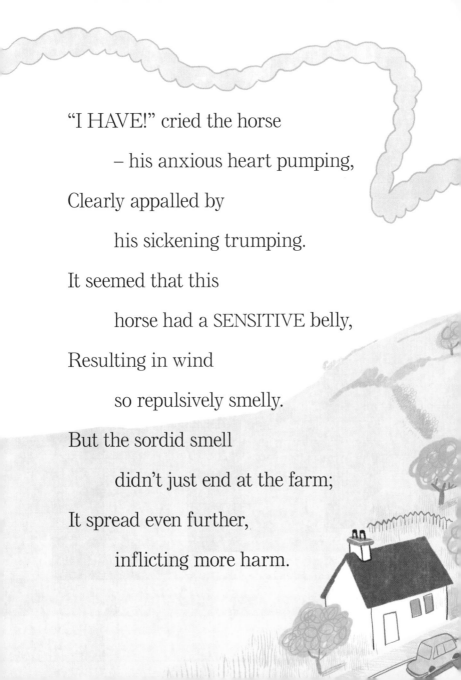

"I HAVE!" cried the horse

      – his anxious heart pumping,

Clearly appalled by

      his sickening trumping.

It seemed that this

      horse had a SENSITIVE belly,

Resulting in wind

      so repulsively smelly.

But the sordid smell

      didn't just end at the farm;

It spread even further,

      inflicting more harm.

It danced through the meadow; then

worked its way down,

Into the valley and onto the town.

The residents screamed and they started retreating.

The Mayor had to call an **EMERGENCY** meeting!

Then, fearing 'A weapon of **reeking** destruction,'

The Mayor picked his phone up, and gave an instruction.

That's when the army turned up on

the scene,

PROFICIENT, RESOURCEFUL and ever

so KEEN.

They pulled on their gas masks and took

to the hill,

Where they marched to the farm to find

Colin and Will.

The sergeant

commanded,

"No need for alarm!"

And he summoned a chopper

to fly to the farm.

The aircraft came quickly, flying

quite low, with big metal storage

container in tow.

The horse was on edge as he watched the

    lights flicker,

And saw that the box had a

    '**BIOHAZARD**' sticker.

The poor horse **gulped**, there was

NOWHERE to hide.

They dropped the container and locked

him inside.

They told farmer Will, it was standard

    routine,

"This horse must remain in complete

    quarantine!"

They locked Colin up for a whole week

    inside,

Until his stomach got well and the **ghastly**

    smell died.

In addition, the Mayor, saw that Will

    signed in ink,

A contract that swore . . .

    THERE'D BE NO FUTURE STINK!

But in order to pledge this, Will had

to say,

That from now on his horse would eat

NOTHING but hay.

We the undersigned
hereby pledge that
Colin the horse will henceforth
eat nothing by hay.

Signed,

Will

Will
the Farmer

Colin
the Horse

The farmer approved, (that was for sure)

So he thought up new ways to make

SUPER-MANURE.

It took him a while, but with sheer

concentration,

He crafted manure to aid germination.

Now he's the maestro of all that he grows;

Inspired by a brainwave right under

his nose.

He created a formula, better than ever . . .

By mixing his livestock's manure

TOGETHER!

As for Colin the horse, well he came to
no harm,

And continues to work and reside on
the farm.

But he's given up dreaming, his mind
doesn't ponder.

He's ever so focused, his thoughts
NEVER wander.

71

He's friends with the

    chickens; still friends

        with the cows,

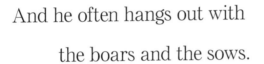

And he often hangs out with

    the boars and the sows.

You'll often see Colin, ploughing

    the field,

Or smiling with **JOY** as he harvests the

    yield.

This horse learned a lesson, from 'life's

    little test'

And decided to stick to a life he

    knows best.

. . . And if **YOU** ever meet him, you'll see

right away . . .

That he's more than content with a life of

JUST hay!

So if life ever deals you a **CURIOUS** thought –

Think of poor Colin and what you've been

taught.

Curiosity bites you and doesn't let go,

Often resulting in **TROUBLES** and WOE.

It can make you believe that the grass is

much greener . . .

But leave you the brunt of your own

misdemeanour.